ARTHUR'S FIRST KISS

逃不掉的亲亲游戏

（美）马克·布朗　绘著

范晓星　译

CHISO 新疆青少年出版社

School was out for the weekend.

"See you at my party tomorrow,"

Francine said to Arthur and Buster.

"Don't forget. It's at my house," said Muffy.

The two girls ran off,
Whispering and giggling.
"So are you REALLY going to kiss
Francine tomorrow?"
Buster asked Arthur.
"What!" yelled Arthur.
"Well, that's what Francine
is telling everyone," said Buster.

"No!" said Arthur.

"I'd rather kiss a frog."

The next day, Arthur got dressed
for the party.
He wore his new yellow sweater
and a red bow tie.

"Oh, you are so handsome,

Lover boy," laughed D.W.

Arthur turned as red as a beet.

7

"I want to go to the party, too," said D.W.

"NO!" said Arthur.

"I'll be your bodyguard," she said. "I'll keep Francine from kissing you."

8

"If you really want to help," said Arthur, "you can take Pal for a walk later."

Arthur walked to Muffy's house
and rang the bell.
"I hope they don't play
that bottle kissing game,"
he said to himself.

WELCOME!

The party was
in the family room.

There were balloons and party hats

and a table with lots of food.

All of Arthur's friends were there.
"Relax," Buster said to Arthur.
"Francine said we won't play
spin-the-bottle."

Francine and Muffy were busy
doing something in the corner.

"I'm writing each boy's name

on a piece of paper for a game,"

Francine said to everyone.

But she didn't write

each boy's name.

She wrote only Arthur's name.

Then she folded the pieces of paper

and put them in a hat.

And Muffy said, "I'm writing

the girls' names."

But she wrote only Francine's name.

"The boy who picks his own name
will be kissed by the girl
who picks her own name!"
said Muffy.
The boys all groaned.

"Here, Arthur, you try first,"
said Muffy.

"I don't want to play,"
said Arthur.

"Oh, come on," said Buster.

"Take a chance."

Arthur picked a piece of paper.

It said "Arthur".

"Oh, no!" he moaned.

Outside, D.W. was walking Pal.

"Muffy lives here," she said.

"Let's do a little party snooping."

D.W. peeked into the window.

She saw Muffy tie a scarf

around Arthur's eyes.

Then Muffy led him to the garage.

"Oh, oh," said D.W.

"The kissing game."

19

D.W. put her ear

next to the window.

She heard Muffy say,

"Now it's the girls' turn.

You go first, Francine."

"Come on, Pal," said D.W.

"Only YOU can save Arthur now."

D.W. ran to the garage.

The door had a tiny flap

for Muffy's cat to go in and out.

D.W. opened the flap

and pushed Pal through it.

Pal was happy to see Arthur.

He jumped on the workbench

and gave Arthur a great big kiss.

Then another and another.

"Stop it, Francine!" said Arthur.

Francine came into the garage
just as Arthur ripped off the scarf.
"It's kissy-kissy time," she said.
"Run for your life!" yelled D.W.
And Arthur did.

Arthur brought a piece of cake

home for D.W.

"Thanks, D.W.," he said.

"You're a great bodyguard."

And he had something

for Pal, too—

a great big kiss.

译文

2. 周末放学的时候，芳馨对亚瑟和巴斯特说：

"明天我的聚会上见。"

3. "不要忘了，聚会在我家举行哦。"玛菲说。

4. 两个小姑娘跑走了，边走边小声嘀咕，还不停地咯咯笑。

"那你明天真的打算亲芳馨喽？"巴斯特问亚瑟。

"你说什么？"亚瑟大喊。

"呃，芳馨就是这样对所有人说的。"巴斯特回答。

5. "不可能！"亚瑟说，"我宁愿亲一只青蛙。"

6. 第二天，亚瑟穿戴整齐，准备去参加聚会。

他穿上新的黄毛衣，戴上红色的小领结。

7. "哇，你好帅呀，万人迷的小帅哥！"朵拉笑着说。

亚瑟的脸"刷"地一下红了。

26

8. "我也想去参加聚会。" 朵拉说。

"不行！" 亚瑟回答。

"我给你当保镖，" 朵拉说，"保证不让芳馨亲到你。"

9. "要是你真想帮忙，" 亚瑟回应，"等会儿就带宝儿去散步吧。"

10. 走到玛菲家，亚瑟按响了门铃。

"但愿他们不玩那个转瓶子的亲亲游戏。" 亚瑟心想。

27

11. 客厅里已经挂满了气球，备好了彩色纸帽，桌子上也摆满了各种好吃的东西。

12. 亚瑟的好朋友们全都到齐了。

"轻松点儿，"巴斯特对亚瑟说，"芳馨说了，我们不会玩那个转瓶子的亲亲游戏。"

13. 芳馨和玛菲正在一旁忙活着什么。

14. "我把每个男生的名字都写在一张小纸条上。"芳馨对大家说。

实际上，她并没有把每个男生的名字都写上，而是只写了亚瑟的名字。

接着，芳馨把这些小纸条一张张叠好，放在一顶帽子里。

玛菲说："我来写所有女生的名字吧。"实际上，她只写了芳馨的名字。

15. "哪个男生抓到写着自己名字的小纸条，就要亲亲那个抓到自己名字的女生！"玛菲又说。

男生们都唉声叹气起来。

16. "来吧，亚瑟，你先来。"玛菲说。

"我不想玩。"亚瑟回答。

"来吧，"巴斯特说，"试一把。"

17. 亚瑟抓了一张纸条，上面写着："亚瑟。"

"哼，我就知道！"他都快哭出来了。

18. 屋外，朵拉正好牵着宝儿在散步。

"玛菲家就在这里，"她说，"咱们偷偷到里面瞧瞧去。"

19. 朵拉趴在窗户边偷偷往里看，只见玛菲往亚瑟眼睛上蒙了一条丝巾，然后把亚瑟带到了车库里。

"哎哟，不好！"朵拉说，"他们在玩亲亲游戏呀！"

20. 朵拉又把耳朵紧贴在窗户上，她听见玛菲说：

"现在该轮到女生抓纸条了。你先来，芳馨。"

"快，宝儿！"朵拉说，"只有你能救哥哥啦！"

21. 朵拉跑到车库外面，看见车库门上有扇专供玛菲家小猫进出的小门。

朵拉打开那扇小门，把宝儿推了进去。

22. 宝儿见到亚瑟可开心了。它跳到工作台上，使劲地亲了亚瑟一下，然后又亲了一下，一下，再一下。

"快停下，芳馨！"亚瑟大喊。

23. 芳馨走进车库的时候，正好亚瑟把蒙住眼睛的丝巾扯了下来。

"亲亲时间到喽！"芳馨说。

"快点逃命！"朵拉大喊。

亚瑟一溜烟儿逃走了。

24. 亚瑟买了一大块蛋糕回家送给朵拉。

"谢谢你，朵拉！"他说，"你真是个称职的保镖。"

亚瑟也给了宝儿一样礼物——一个大大的、香香的亲亲。